The

United Nations

Global Leadership

International Security

Peacekeeping and Peace-Building Around the World

by Autumn Libal

Mason Crest Publishers

Philadelphia

Mason Crest Publishers Inc.
370 Reed Road
Broomall, Pennsylvania 19008
(866) MCP-BOOK (toll free)

First printing
1 2 3 4 5 6 7 8 9 10
    Library of Congress Cataloging-in-Publication Data

Libal, Autumn.
  International security : peacekeeping and peace-building around the world / by Autumn Libal.
      p. cm. — (The United Nations–global leadership)
  Includes bibliographical references and index.
  ISBN 1-4222-0071-X ISBN 1-4222-0065-5 (series)
  1. United Nations—Juvenile literature. 2. United Nations—Peacekeeping forces—Juvenile literature.
3. Peace—Juvenile literature. 4. Security, International—Juvenile literature. I. Title. II. Series.
  JZ4984.6.L53 2007
  341.7—dc22
                            2006001477

Interior design by Benjamin Stewart.
Interiors produced by Harding House Publishing Service, Inc.
www.hardinghousepages.com
Cover design by Peter Culatta.
Printed in the Hashemite Kingdom of Jordan.

Contents

Introduction
by Dr. Bruce Russett

The United Nations was founded in 1945 by the victors of World War II. They hoped the new organization could learn from the mistakes of the League of Nations that followed World War I—and prevent another war.

The United Nations has not been able to bring worldwide peace; that would be an unrealistic hope. But it has contributed in important ways to the world's experience of more than sixty years without a new world war. Despite its flaws, the United Nations has contributed to peace.

Like any big organization, the United Nations is composed of many separate units with different jobs. These units make three different kinds of contributions. The most obvious to students in North America and other democracies are those that can have a direct and immediate impact for peace.

Especially prominent is the Security Council, which is the only UN unit that can authorize the use of military force against countries and can require all UN members to cooperate in isolating an aggressor country's economy. In the Security Council, each of the big powers—Britain, China, France, Russia, and the United States—can veto any proposed action. That's because the founders of United Nations recognized that if the Council tried to take any military action against the strong opposition of a big power it would result in war. As a result, the United Nations was often sidelined during the Cold War era. Since the end of the Cold War in 1990, however, the Council has authorized many military actions, some directed against specific aggressors but most intended as more neutral peacekeeping efforts. Most of its peacekeeping efforts have been to end civil wars rather than wars between countries. Not all have succeeded, but many have. The United Nations Secretary-General also has had an important role in mediating some conflicts.

UN units that promote trade and economic development make a different kind of contribution. Some help to establish free markets for greater prosperity, or like the UN Development Programme, provide economic and technical assistance to reduce poverty in poor countries. Some are especially concerned with environmental problems or health issues. For example, the World Health Organization and UNICEF deserve great credit for eliminating the deadly disease of smallpox from the world. Poor countries especially support the United Nations for this reason. Since many wars, within and between countries, stem from economic deprivation, these efforts make an important indirect contribution to peace.

Still other units make a third contribution: they promote human rights. The High Commission for Refugees, for example, has worked to ease the distress of millions of refugees who have fled their countries to escape from war and political persecution. A special unit of the Secretary-General's office has supervised and assisted free elections in more than ninety countries. It tries to establish stable and democratic governments in newly independent countries or in countries where the people have defeated a dictatorial government. Other units promote the rights of women, children, and religious and ethnic minorities. The General Assembly provides a useful setting for debate on these and other issues.

These three kinds of action—to end violence, to reduce poverty, and to promote social and political justice—all make a contribution to peace. True peace requires all three, working together.

The UN does not always succeed: like individuals, it makes mistakes . . . and it often learns from its mistakes. Despite the United Nations' occasional stumbles, over the years it has grown and moved forward. These books will show you how.

The United Nations has worked for peace for more than sixty years.

Chapter **1**

The Vision: The Formation of the UN and Its Charter

T*he only true basis of enduring peace is the willing cooperation of free peoples in a world in which, relieved of the menace of aggression, all may enjoy economic and social security; it is our intention to work together, and with other free peoples, both in war and peace, to this end.* (From "The Declaration of St. James's Palace" signed in London by Great Britain, Canada, Australia, New Zealand, the Union of South Africa, and the exiled governments of Belgium, Czechoslovakia, Greece, Luxembourg, the Netherlands, Norway, Poland, Yugoslavia, and free France during the height of the Second World War.)

International Security: Peacekeeping and Peace-Building Around the World

The Goal of World Peace

In 1945, the United Nations formed with one overwhelming goal in mind: to create a world of peace and security for all people. The First World War taught, and the Second World War reinforced, a powerful lesson to world leaders: ripples of discontent in one part of the world can cause waves of unrest across the globe. In the twentieth century, it became clear that the world had profoundly changed. No one could remain isolated within national boundaries. Modern industry, technology, and economy were shaping a new world order in which all countries had a stake. New military capabilities held potential for mass destruction like never before. With the advent of the atomic bomb, used in the closing days of World War II, even total obliteration seemed possible.

Amid great fear, however, **visionary** world leaders recognized that these uncertain times also held opportunity, the opportunity for the world's people to come together. The formation of the United Nations was a supreme act of hope arising from a belief that, with the participation and cooperation of all nations, a lasting peace could be achieved for all peoples. It was not the first attempt at an international organization dedicated to peace. The most recent attempt had been the failed League of Nations, formed after World War I and proven inadequate by World War II. The United Nations sought to succeed where the League of Nations and others had failed. Never before had humanity united in such a way, and all hoped it spelled a better future for the world.

The Charter of the United Nations

Throughout World War II, the leaders of numerous countries met to discuss how a lasting peace could be maintained if and when the Axis powers were defeated. In 1942, twenty-six nations signed a Declaration of United Nations, and on June 26, 1945, with defeat of the Axis powers finally at hand, representatives from fifty countries met in San Francisco to sign a historic treaty that would guide the newly formed organization in matters of world affairs. It was called the Charter of the United Nations, and it opened with the following **preamble**:

WE THE PEOPLES OF THE UNITED NATIONS DETERMINED

to save succeeding generations from the scourge of war; which twice in our lifetime has brought untold sorrow to mankind, and

The Atlantic Charter meeting took place on HMS Prince of Wales *in 1941.*

The chapters of the Charter of the United Nations are:

Chapter I: Purposes and Principles
Chapter II: Membership
Chapter III: Organs
Chapter IV: The General Assembly
Chapter V: The Security Council
Chapter VI: Pacific Settlement of Disputes
Chapter VII: Action with Respect to Threats to the Peace, Breaches of the Peace, and Acts of Aggression
Chapter VIII: Regional Arrangements
Chapter IX: International Economic and Social Co-Operation
Chapter X: The Economic and Social Council
Chapter XI: Declaration Regarding Non-Self-Governing Territories
Chapter XII: International Trusteeship System
Chapter XIII: The Trusteeship Council
Chapter XIV: The International Court of Justice
Chapter XV: The Secretariat
Chapter XVI: Miscellaneous Provisions
Chapter XVII: Transitional Security Arrangements
Chapter XVIII: Amendments
Chapter XIX: Ratification and Signature

to reaffirm faith in fundamental human rights, in the dignity and worth of the human person, in the equal rights of men and women and of nations large and small, and

to establish conditions under which justice and respect for the obligations arising from treaties and other sources of international law can be maintained, and

to promote social progress and better standards of life in larger freedom,

AND FOR THESE ENDS

to practice tolerance and live together in peace with one another as good neighbors, and

DECLARATION

BY UNITED NATIONS

The United Nations was born on January 1, 1942, when twenty-six governments signed the Declaration of the United Nations.

During an early humanitarian effort, UN workers used poison to combat locusts in Morocco.

to unite our strength to maintain international peace and security, and

to ensure, by the acceptance of principles and the institution of methods, that armed force shall not be used, save in the common interest, and

to employ international machinery for the promotion of the economic and social advancement of all peoples,

HAVE RESOLVED TO COMBINE OUR EFFORTS TO ACCOMPLISH THESE AIMS

Accordingly, our respective Governments, through representatives assembled in the city of San Francisco, who have exhibited their full powers found to be in good and due form, have agreed to the present Charter of the United Nations and do hereby establish an international organization to be known as the United Nations.

The document that follows is made up of nineteen chapters consisting of 111 articles that guide the world in matters of peace, security, **humanitarian** affairs, and international cooperation.

On October 24, 1945, the treaty officially went into effect, and the United Nations was born. According to Chapter I, Article 1 of the charter, the purposes of the United Nations are:

1. *To maintain international peace and security, and to that end: to take effective collective measures for the prevention and removal of threats to the peace, and for the suppression of acts of aggression or other breaches of the peace, and to bring about by peaceful means, and in conformity with the principles of justice and international law, adjustment or settlement of international disputes or situations which might lead to a breach of the peace;*
2. *To develop friendly relations among nations based on respect for the principle of equal rights and self-determination of peoples, and to take other appropriate measures to strengthen universal peace;*
3. *To achieve international co-operation in solving international problems of an economic, social, cultural, or humanitarian character, and in promoting and encouraging respect for human rights and for fundamental freedoms for all without distinction as to race, sex, language, or religion; and*

In the Congo, volunteers signed up to work on UN humanitarian projects.

4. To be a center for harmonizing the actions of nations in the attainment of these common ends.

Chapter I, Article 2 of the charter, describes the principles that all UN Member states must follow as they pursue the purposes stated in Article 1. They are:

1. The Organization is based on the principle of the sovereign equality of all its Members.

2. All Members, in order to ensure to all of them the rights and benefits resulting from membership, shall fulfill in good faith the obligations assumed by them in accordance with the present Charter.

3. All Members shall settle their international disputes by peaceful means in such a manner that international peace and security, and justice, are not endangered.

4. All Members shall refrain in their international relations from the threat or use of force against the territorial integrity or political independence of any state, or in any other manner inconsistent with the Purposes of the United Nations.

5. All Members shall give the United Nations every assistance in any action it takes in accordance with the present Charter, and shall refrain from giving assistance to any state against which the United Nations is taking preventive or enforcement action.

6. The Organization shall ensure that states which are not Members of the United Nations act in accordance with these Principles so far as may be necessary for the maintenance of international peace and security.

7. Nothing contained in the present Charter shall authorize the United Nations to intervene in matters which are essentially within the domestic jurisdiction of any state or shall require the Members to submit such matters to settlement under the present Charter; but this principle shall not prejudice the application of enforcement measures under Chapter VII.

The UN headquarters in New York City

Chapter **2**

The Body: The UN's Organizational Structure

The Headquarters

The UN headquarters is located in New York City. Geneva, Switzerland; Vienna, Austria; Nairobi, Kenya; and many other cities around the world are also home to UN offices. As an organization, the United Nations has six main bodies: the General Assembly, the Security Council, the Economic and Social Council, the Trusteeship Council, the International Court of Justice, and the Secretariat. In addition, there are numerous organizations, called the UN Family, that fall under the UN umbrella.

The General Assembly

When the United Nations formed over sixty years ago, the General Assembly consisted of fifty-one members—the original fifty participants from the San Francisco conference, plus Poland, which was recognized as a founding member when it too signed the charter on October 24. Today, representatives from 191 nations—almost every nation in the world—make up the General Assembly. In this assembly, often called a ***parliament*** of the world, all nations are treated equally; each country has one vote no matter how big, small, powerful, or weak that country may be.

The General Assembly can be thought of as a court of world opinion. Unlike a court of law, there is nothing legally binding about the decisions the General Assembly makes. Nevertheless, since its pronouncements carry the weight of world opinion, the assembly can have considerable influence. Each year, the General Assembly makes numerous decisions on far-ranging issues such as world health, environmental protection, economic aid, the promotion of democratic principles, and many more. Depending on the type of issue being discussed, a majority vote, two-thirds majority, or assembly ***consensus*** may be sought to approve a measure. The General Assembly's annual session runs from September to December, but emergency sessions can be called at any point during the year.

The Security Council

Matters of international peace and security are entrusted to the UN Security Council, a council of five permanent and ten regularly elected members. The Security Council's permanent members are China, France, the Russian Federation, the United Kingdom, and the United States. These members all hold ***veto*** power over decisions the council makes (except decisions on procedural questions). The other ten members are elected by the General Assembly for two-year terms. Council resolutions require nine votes to pass—the votes of all five permanent members plus at least four of the nonpermanent members.

The Security Council's actions are governed by Chapters VI, VII, VIII, and XII of the charter. The Security Council has some powerful tools for enforcing its rulings. When a matter of international peace and security arises, the council firsts seeks to end the dispute through peaceful negotiations. When such negotiations fail, the council will consider more forceful measures such as economic ***sanctions*** or arms ***embargos***. When these measures fail, military action will be considered. Using military force is always meant to be a last resort, used only if every possible option for a peaceful resolution has failed.

A meeting of the UN Security Council

The Trusteeship Council in session

The Economic and Social Council

The fifty-four-member Economic and Social Council oversees numerous UN organizations and also works with many nongovernmental organizations to conduct economic, social, cultural, educational, and health-related projects around the world. Members of the council are elected by the General Assembly to three-year terms. Some of the organizations governed by the council are the Commission on Human Rights, Commission on the Status of Women, Commission on Science and Technology for Development, and Commission on Sustainable Development.

The Trusteeship Council

Unlike the other major UN bodies, the Trusteeship Council no longer has a sustained role to play in the United Nations. When it was first formed, the council oversaw eleven Trust Territories, territories that were without self-government after World War II. By 1994, however, all eleven of these territories achieved self-governance, independence, or joined other independent nations. Its mandate now achieved, the Trusteeship Council suspended regular operation on November 1, 1994.

The International Court of Justice

The International Court of Justice, often called the World Court, sits at the Peace Palace in The Hague, Netherlands. The primary role of the court is to pass judgments on legal disputes between **states** (only states, not individuals, can bring questions to the court). Unlike other courts, participation at the World Court is voluntary. However, once a state agrees to bring a matter to the court, it is obligated to comply with the court's decision. If a state refuses to comply, the other party may appeal to the UN Security Council for assistance in achieving compliance.

The other major role of the court is to advise specific international bodies and agencies by giving opinions on legal matters. For instance, when the UN Security Council has a question regarding an international legal matter pertinent to its work, it may seek an advisory opinion from the International Court of Justice.

The UN General Assembly and Security Council are in charge of electing the court's fifteen judges. Each judge sits for a nine-year term. Judges come from all over the world, but to be considered for the World Court, judges must be qualified to sit at the highest judicial level in their own countries or have exceptional knowledge and abilities in the field of international law. Since

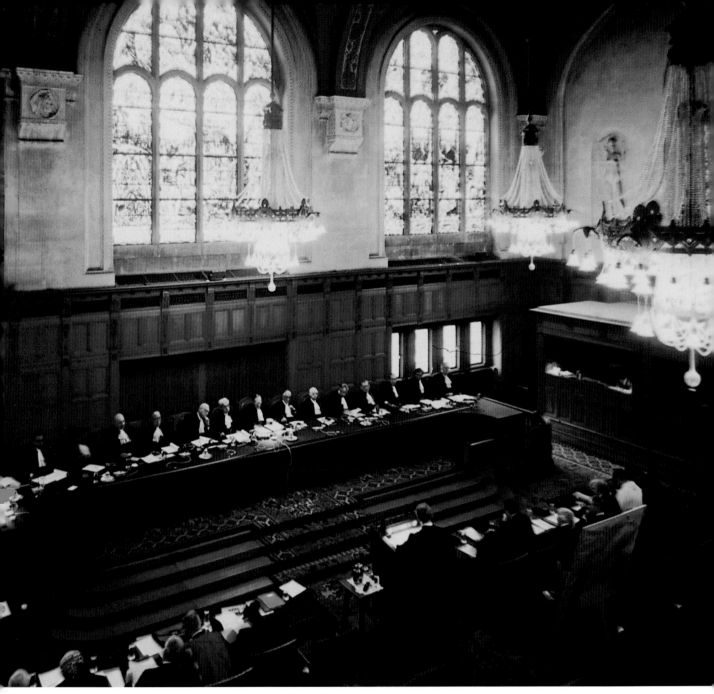

The International Court of Justice meets at The Hague.

A UN session in Cairo, Egypt

its inception in 1946, the court has made judgments and delivered opinions on wide-ranging issues such as territorial disputes, *maritime* boundaries, hostage-taking, and economic rights.

The Secretariat

The Secretariat is by far the largest UN body. Its regular staff consists of nearly 9,000 employees from approximately 170 nations. They work at the UN headquarters in New York City, as well as at UN offices in hundreds of other cities around the world. Collectively, these people are the organization's administrative staff—they are the ones who keep the United Nations running and do the work necessary to turn the General Assembly's decisions into reality. At any given time, thousands of additional people are employed in UN projects across the globe.

People employed as members of the Secretariat perform a huge variety of duties. Some are translators facilitating communication between UN members with different languages. Others are statisticians collecting information and preparing reports on issues like the progress of human rights, women's economic contributions, or *sustainable* development in specific nations. Some

The UN Secretariat and General Assembly buildings in New York City

are running peacekeeping missions. Others are arranging the UN's numerous conferences. And the list goes on.

Every five years, the General Assembly elects a secretary-general to run the Secretariat. The position of secretary-general is a demanding job that requires the highest level of *diplomatic* skill. As the only person *vested* with the power to speak on behalf of the entire United Nations, the secretary-general must act as the UN's ambassador to the world. In addition, the secretary-general is often called on to act as a negotiator between countries. The secretary-general, and all members of the Secretariat, swear an oath to work only on behalf of the United Nations and not use their position in this international organization to attempt to further any individual country's interests.

The UN Family

The "UN Family" or "UN System" are names given to a group of specialized agencies, UN offices, programs, and funds that function with or under the guidance of the United Nations. Fourteen independent organizations have cooperative agreements with the United Nations. Among them are the International Monetary Fund, the World Bank, and the World Health Organization. A number of other major offices, programs, or funds also report either to the General Assembly or the Economic and Social Council. Among them are the United Nations Children's Fund (UNICEF), the UN High Commissioner for Refugees (UNHCR), and the UN Development Program (UNDP).

The UN works to control the use of weapons around the world.

Chapter

3

The Tools: How the UN Promotes Peace and Security

Most responsibilities for the maintenance of international peace lie with the Security Council. Chapter VII, "Action with Respect to Threats to the Peace, Breaches of the Peace, and Acts of Aggression," of the UN charter gives details as to how the Security Council functions in situations that threaten the peace. Particularly important are Articles 39, 41, and 42.

Article 39:

The Security Council shall determine the existence of any threat to the peace, breach of the peace, or act of aggression and shall make recommendations, or decide what measures shall be taken in accordance with Articles 41 and 42, to maintain or restore international peace and security.

Article 41:

The Security Council may decide what measures not involving the use of armed force are to be employed to give effect to its decisions, and it may call upon the Members of the United Nations to apply such measures. These may include complete or partial interruption of economic relations and of rail, sea, air, postal, telegraphic, radio, and other means of communication, and the severance of diplomatic relations.

Article 42:

Should the Security Council consider that measures provided for in Article 41 would be inadequate or have proved to be inadequate, it may take such action by air, sea, or land forces as may be necessary to maintain or restore international peace and security. Such action may include demonstrations, blockades, and other operations by air, sea, or land forces of Members of the United Nations.

The UN's and Security Council's responsibilities toward maintaining peace outlined in Chapter VII and elsewhere in the charter are carried out in specific ways. There are four major categories of actions the United Nations takes to promote peace around the world: ***disarmament***, peacemaking, peace-building, and peacekeeping.

Disarmament

Although not specifically called for in the charter, one very important way the United Nations works to promote peace is through disarmament efforts. Too often in history, states have used their weapons stockpiles, rather than diplomacy, to do their talking. During the cold war, for example, the world saw how dangerous these arms races could be. Now the United Nations works to decrease the number of weapons, large and small, around the world. The UN disarmament efforts are also concerned with the types of weapons states use, encouraging states to cease the development, manufacture, and use of certain types of weapons, especially those that cause great harm to civilian populations. The United Nations hopes to one day see all weapons of mass destruction eliminated. It is also working hard to halt illegal weapons trade.

Stockpiled missiles do not promote peace.

In the 1960s, protestors marched outside the United Nations in New York City, insisting that the UN do what it could to stop the United States from resuming its testing of the atomic bomb.

The NPT does not mean that our world is free of nuclear weapons. Submarines with nuclear capabilities are just one form of nuclear weapon possessed by several nations.

One of the UN's greatest disarmament successes is the Treaty on the Non-Proliferation of Nuclear Weapons (NPT). Countries began signing the NPT in 1968. Today, the treaty has 187 members, including the five nuclear powers: China, France, the Russian Federation, the United Kingdom, and the United States. Parties to the treaty are permitted to develop and share nuclear technology for peaceful purposes, such as the creation of electricity, but promise not to develop or pursue the production of nuclear arms. Those who already had such weapons when they signed the treaty promised to dismantle those weapons. The fact that this treaty exists and so many countries are party to it, however, does not mean that our world is now free of nuclear weapons. Although all five nuclear powers have pledged to dismantle their stockpiles, there is no timetable for achieving this goal, a situation some observers see as a major flaw in the treaty. Furthermore, a number of countries in the world are currently pursuing or are greatly suspected of intending to pursue the production of nuclear arms.

In 1996, the passage of the Comprehensive Nuclear-Test-Ban Treaty (CTBT), which bans all nuclear explosions, built upon the NPT. The treaty currently has 175 member states, including all five nuclear powers. The International Atomic Energy Agency (IAEA) oversees compliance with the NPT, CTBT, and similar treaties and agreements regarding nuclear weapons. Part of the UN Family, the IAEA is based in Vienna and works for the safe and peaceful development and use of nuclear technologies.

Also part of the UN Family is the Organization for the Prohibition of Chemical Weapons (OPCW). Similar to the IAEA, this international organization works toward the destruction of existing chemical weapons, monitors the chemical industry to help assure that commercial chemicals are not used to make weapons, and promotes the peaceful use of chemistry.

Not all the UN's disarmament efforts, however, are focused on weapons with the potential for mass destruction. In fact, some of the most destructive weapons in terms of causing deaths and horrific, permanent injuries are actually quite small and claim their victims one at a time. According to the International Campaign to Ban Landmines, there are between fifteen and twenty thousand land mine casualties each year—equal to about two every hour. Although land mines are usually laid during conflicts, the mines are almost never removed when warring factions achieve

A half-buried land mine in Cambodia is a horrific reminder of the war in Southeast Asia.

CHEMICAL WEAPON
medium range
<120 million people

Chemical weapons pose a danger to the Earth's people.

A 1943 exhibit in New York City's Rockefeller Center honors the UN's peacekeeping contributions.

peace. Therefore, the majority of land mine casualties today actually happen to civilians, many of them children, in countries that are now at peace.

The United Nations is working hard to change the world's record when it comes to land mine casualties. In 1997, it passed the Convention on the Prohibition of the Use, Stockpiling, Production and Transfer of Antipersonnel Mines and on Their Destruction, called the Ottawa Convention for short. This treaty, which more than 120 countries have signed, deals with halting the production, trade, and use of land mines and providing aid to people who have been injured by them. However, there are some very important holdouts to the Ottawa Convention. More than forty countries have not signed. Notable among them are the United States, the Russian Federation, China, and a number of countries with some of the world's worst land mine problems, including Iraq, Nepal, and Sri Lanka.

Peacemaking

Whether armed conflict has already broken out or disputing parties are simply in danger of picking up arms, the United Nations often intervenes in the hopes of making peace. Such efforts rely on diplomacy, with the United Nations either trying to bring both sides to the bargaining table, or acting as a *liaison* between arguing factions. The responsibilities that come with peacemaking are overseen by the UN Department of Political Affairs, which is currently headed by Under-Secretary-General Ibrahim A. Gambari. The UN's peacemaking attempts are always based on diplomacy. The term "peace enforcement" is used to describe situations in which force must be used to bring an end to conflict.

Peacemaking efforts, as well as all the UN's efforts to ensure peace and security around the world, can be dangerous for those involved on the ground. Often with very little protection, UN workers face what are literally war zones, and move between fighting parties searching for a peaceful solution that can put an end to the bloodshed happening around them.

Peace-Building

Going hand-in-hand with peacemaking and also overseen by the Department of Political Affairs is peace-building. For years, the United Nations acted much like the world's fire station, racing to put out blazes before they spread out of control. Any firefighter will tell you, however, that the best way to fight fires is to prevent them from starting in the first place. Today, the United Nations is realizing that lasting peace cannot be achieved by simply putting out the fires of conflict once they ignite; peacemaking alone is not enough. Instead, steps must be taken to ensure that those fires never light. For this reason, greater efforts are being placed on developing the conditions that promote peace-a process called peace-building.

One major part of peace-building is something called structural prevention. Structural prevention attempts to address the root causes of conflict by building the conditions that promote peace in the long term—conditions like **civil law** and order, free elections, sustainable economies, and adequate access to essential goods and services like food, water, and health care. These efforts to lay the foundations for peace by building strong communities, societies, and nations are quickly becoming a major focus of the United Nations.

In an area that is experiencing great hardship, socioeconomic inequalities, weak government, or other conditions that often lead to conflict, the United Nations may engage in structural prevention activities before a conflict even arises. When the undercurrents of conflict are already stirring, UN personnel will likely call on other peace-building tools. One extremely important tool for peace-building is preventive diplomacy—negotiation done in an effort to keep a disagreement or conflict from **escalating**. Some of the most important people working in preventive diplomacy around the world are the UN **Envoys** and Special Representatives of the Secretary-General. These envoys and representatives are stationed in trouble areas. They are individuals with years of experience in political negotiations, and their vast mediation skills are used to negotiate all kinds of tense situations.

Sometimes the United Nations feels it must go beyond preventive diplomacy to keep an emerging conflict at bay; in such a situation it may, with the consent of the host country, turn to preventive deployment. UN peacekeeping troops would then be sent to the area, not to engage in any fighting, but to act as a type of human buffer between parties in danger of picking up arms. The hope is that the mere presence of the UN troops will be enough to discourage fighting and encourage an atmosphere of trust and stability. To date, preventive deployment has only been used twice: in the former Yugoslav Republic of Macedonia and in the Central African Republic.

Like preventive diplomacy and preventive deployment, preventive disarmament may also be used as part of peace-building efforts. Preventive disarmament entails collecting and destroying small arms in areas of high tension. As the UN Department of Political Affairs states on its Web site, "Destroying yesterday's weapons prevents their being used in tomorrow's wars."

Peace-building efforts may be undertaken before any conflict breaks out, but they are also important to ensuring that a resolved conflict doesn't recur. In fact, many of the UN peace-building efforts take place in post-conflict situations. For example, civil wars, once ended, often begin

Diplomacy is one of the UN's most effective methods for building peace.

UN peacekeepers may be called in anywhere in the world where there is violence and political unrest.

again within a relatively short period of time. Some of the underlying causes that make such a conflict likely to recur are poverty, social inequality, and human-rights violations. According to retired UN Under-Secretary-General for Political Affairs Kieran Prendergast:

> What is more important [than ending the immediate violence] is that people develop the ways and means to live together peacefully. For that, they need good institutions, such as justice systems and police forces that former adversaries can trust and uphold.

Peacekeeping

Whereas peacemaking relies on diplomacy, peacekeeping, which is overseen by the Security Council, is often a matter that requires military intervention. But peacekeeping and peacemaking do go hand-in-hand. For example, UN peacekeeping forces may be called in to maintain calm and order on the ground so that peacemakers can safely do their work. A wide range of activities, from military personnel policing a cease-fire to civilian workers monitoring elections, are included in peacekeeping. Peacekeeping forces are not sent to intervene in a conflict unless the host country consents to their presence, and usually the consent of the other parties involved in the conflict is also sought.

Even though peacekeeping often involves military personnel, it is important not to confuse peacekeeping operations with combat operations. The armed military personnel deployed on a peacekeeping mission are not meant to fight on behalf of any side involved in the conflict. They are meant to help create the atmosphere that will allow for peace and security. In doing so, they are ordered to use their weapons only for self-defense and then with utmost restraint. Peacekeeping missions of the past have often been criticized for not using their weapons to intervene when civilians are harmed in conflicts. However, peacekeepers are present with the consent of the countries in which they work, and if they began using their weapons to intervene in conflicts, countries might cease allowing peacekeeping missions to go forward. In that event, UN peacekeeping as a whole would be undermined. Sometimes the international community may be at fault for not committing appropriate military intervention to a given conflict, but such interventions are beyond the scope of peacekeeping.

Since the first peacekeeping mission was launched in 1948, the United Nations has headed fifty-four peacekeeping operations. Some operations are completed within a number of months, while others are ongoing years after the initial conflict has ended. For example, the peacekeeping mission that monitors the cease-fire between India and Pakistan in the State of Jammu and

Here UN peacekeepers destroy weapons surrendered by resistance forces.

Kashmir has existed since 1949. The peacekeeping mission in Cyprus that works to maintain peaceful relations between the Greek Cypriot and Turkish Cypriot communities began in 1964 and continues today. Currently, the United Nations has sixteen peacekeeping operations being carried out around the world: eight in Africa, one in the Americas, one in Asia, three in Europe, and three in the Middle East.

Despite its name, peacekeeping is often not peaceful. UN peacekeepers are sometimes targeted for violence, especially if one party to a conflict does not approve of their presence. According to the United Nations Department of Peacekeeping Operations, to date 2,033 peacekeepers have been killed in the line of duty. In fact, the United Nations has not had a year free of peacekeeper fatalities since 1955.

Africa is a continent filled with unrest.

Chapter

A History of Peacemaking and Peacekeeping

Past Missions: An Overview

Africa is by far the continent that has seen the most UN peacekeeping operations. Fifteen missions have occurred: in Angola (four missions), Central African Republic, Chad/Libya, the Congo, Liberia, Mozambique, Namibia, Rwanda, Rwanda/Uganda, Sierra Leone, and Somalia (two missions).

The Americas have also had their share of UN peacekeeping missions. Eight were carried out here in the past. They were in Central America, the Dominican Republic, El Salvador, Guatemala, and Haiti (four missions).

In Asia and the Pacific, peacekeeping missions have been carried out in East Timor (two missions), Cambodia (two missions), Afghanistan/Pakistan, India/Pakistan, Tajikistan, and West New Guinea.

The United Nations has had seven past peacekeeping operations in Europe. These have mostly been concentrated in the region formerly known as Yugoslavia. They have been in Croatia (three missions), former Yugoslavia, the former Yugoslav Republic of Macedonia, the Prevlaka Peninsula, and Bosnia and Herzegovina.

There have been six past Middle East peacekeeping operations. Their locations were in Iran/Iraq, Lebanon, Yemen, and Iraq/Kuwait.

The United Nations began carrying out operations to promote peace and security around the world in 1947. However, these missions would not be referred to as "peacekeeping" for about a decade. The first time the term "peacekeeping" was officially used was during the Suez Crisis of 1956.

UNEF I

The Suez Crisis was a serious test of the UN's ability to follow through with meaningful action when its member states violated its core principles, and it involved some of the organization's most influential members. Until July 1956, British and French companies had jointly operated Egypt's valuable Suez Canal. The canal connects the Mediterranean to the Red Sea, making it one of the most important maritime passageways in the world. In the 1950s, the canal was bringing in millions of dollars in profits a year, but since the companies running the canal were foreign owned, Egypt saw almost none of the profits. The Egyptian president, Gamal Abdel-Nasser, decided to nationalize the canal companies, meaning the canal would no longer be privately owned and operated; it would be controlled by the Egyptian government.

Not surprisingly, Nasser's decision infuriated Great Britain and France. Tensions ran high, and in October, the UN Security Council passed a resolution that outlined how the canal should be administered. Unknown to the Security Council, however, Britain and France entered into secret negotiations to regain control of the canal, and they invited Egypt's archenemy, Israel, to participate. Behind closed doors, an invasion was planned. Israel would attack from the east, entering Sinai and the Gaza Strip. While Egypt was busy defending itself from Israel's invasion, Britain and France would swoop in and seize the canal. On October 29, the plan went into effect.

In the 1950s, the Suez Canal was a source of conflict between Egypt, Great Britain, and France.

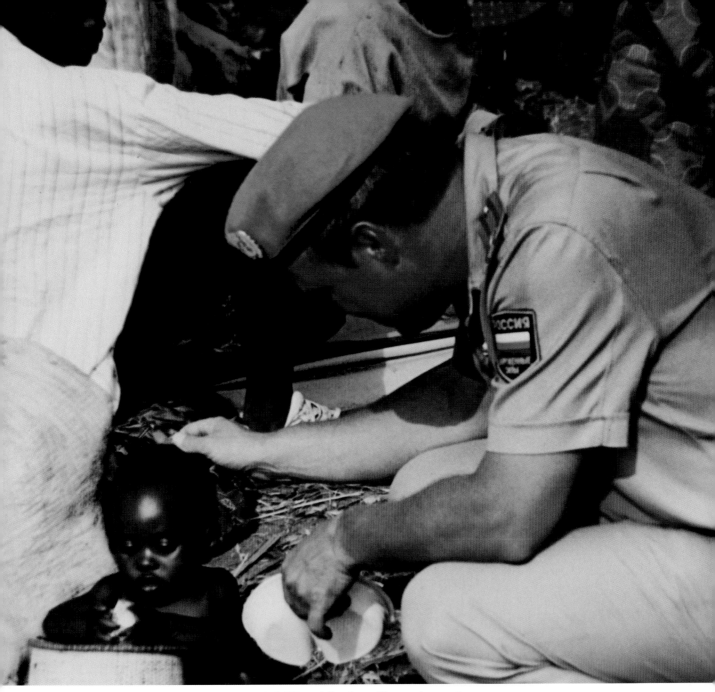

A Russian UNIMIR soldier in a Rwandan refugee camp

Back at UN headquarters, the Security Council was in crisis. The United States was enraged that Britain and France had secretly planned military action. To make matters worse, they had involved Israel, which the United States supplied with military equipment. The entire situation, though focused on the relatively small Suez area, could ultimately involve the world. The United States was implicated through its friendship with Israel, and Egypt could easily turn to its friend (and the United States' ultimate foe), the Soviet Union. With Britain and France each armed with veto power at the Security Council's negotiating table, the body that was supposed to ensure international peace and security was rendered completely powerless.

With the Security Council unable to offer a solution, the issue was turned over to the General Assembly. Meeting in emergency sessions, the General Assembly called for an immediate halt to hostilities and withdrawal of all foreign troops from Egyptian territory. The United Nations Emergency Force (UNEF) was formed to oversee the withdrawal.

UNEF I, as the first UN peacekeeping force, was conceived differently than peace operations of the past, and it set standards for peace operations of the future. It went forward with the consent of all parties involved in the conflict. The force was armed but charged to use their weapons only in self-defense and, if required to use their weapons, to do so with utmost restraint—restrictions that continue to be placed on peacekeeping missions today. UNEF I peacekeepers oversaw the removal of occupying forces and helped maintain stability in the region for approximately ten years.

At its height, UNEF I consisted of 6,073 military personnel supported by international and local civilian staff. It suffered 110 fatalities—109 military personnel and one civilian staff member. In 1967, UNEF I ended when Egypt withdrew its consent for the peacekeeping program.

UNOMUR and UNAMIR

The United Nations' most catastrophic peacekeeping failure occurred in the African country of Rwanda in 1994. Rwanda has a long history of ethnic tensions between its minority Tutsi and majority Hutu populations. The two ethnic groups are in most respects difficult or impossible to tell apart: they have the same language, live in the same areas, and share many cultural traditions. However, when Belgians colonized the country in the early twentieth century, they favored the Tutsis, giving them better jobs and educational opportunities. In so doing, they created the embers of resentment that would one day burst into *genocide*.

The Hutu majority suffered under Belgium's rule, and often laid blame on their Tutsi countrymen. When Rwanda was granted independence in 1962, the Hutus gained control of the government. From that point forward, whenever a crisis ensued, the Tutsis were used as scapegoats. Ethnic tensions continued to worsen decades after the colonialists departed.

By 1990, tensions were boiling over. Tutsi refugees in neighboring Uganda had formed a rebel army called the Rwandese Patriotic Front (RPF). Some moderate Hutus also supported the RPF, but for the radical "Hutu Power" movement, the rebels were more fuel for the anti-Tutsi fire.

Fighting between the RPF and the armed forces of the Rwandan government was ongoing until July 1992, when a cease-fire was enacted. This precarious peace, however, lasted less than six months. By early February 1993, hostilities had resumed, and anti-Tutsi **propaganda** was raging in Rwanda. In June, the United Nations' first intervention began with the United Nations Observer Mission Uganda-Rwanda (UNOMUR), which sent military observers to the Ugandan side of the Uganda-Rwanda border to verify that no military assistance reached Rwanda.

In August 1993, a peace agreement was signed, and in October of that year, the United Nations deployed a second peacekeeping force, the United Nations Assistance Mission for Rwanda (UNAMIR) to assist in the implementation of that agreement.

From the beginning, UNAMIR was hampered by a lack of commitment on the part of UN Member States. At first, only Belgium and Bangladesh responded, and the mission was forced to operate with a fraction of the troops it was supposed to have. During that time, Force Commander Major-General Romeo A. Dallaire communicated his concerns to the United Nations that tensions were mounting and something catastrophic could be on its way. His concerns fell on deaf ears. Neither the United Nations nor its Member States responded to Dallaire's requests for further aid. It took a full five months before the total 2,548 troops could be assembled, and in the interim, the potential for success under the peace agreement deteriorated.

April 1994 saw the final straw in the tense situation. Rwandan president Juvenal Habyarimana, a Hutu, was killed when his plane crashed as it landed in the nation's capital, Kigali. Officially, the cause of the fatal crash is still unknown, but unofficially it is widely believed that Hutu-power extremists shot down the plane to spark a civil war.

With the president dead, no one could rein in Rwanda's bloodthirsty military. The prime minister and other politicians in favor of peace and restraint were killed. UNAMIR peacekeepers were also targeted. But those who were targeted like no one else were the Tutsis. Suddenly it was as if most of the country had lost its mind, and mass murders of Tutsis and moderate Hutus began. The carnage that ensued was beyond comprehension. Machete-wielding gangs murdered people in their homes, in schools, in churches, in the streets; virtually no place was safe, and bodies lay everywhere.

As the massacre spread, countries began withdrawing their troops from UNAMIR, and on April 21, rather than voting to intervene to stop the violence in Rwanda, the UN Security Council

The land of Rwanda saw some of the twentieth century's worst violence.

The crushed skull of a genocide victim is a grisly reminder of the UN's failure to prevent the atrocity that took place in Rwanda.

voted to reduce the size of UNAMIR from 2,548 to just 270. The remaining UNAMIR peacekeepers, though able to protect a small number of refugees at secured sites, were basically helpless. Charged to only use their weapons in self-defense and hopelessly outnumbered, the peacekeepers could do virtually nothing as the bodies piled up around them. In May, all-out genocide raging in the country, the Security Council reversed its decision, increasing UNAMIR's strength to 5,500, but it took six months to assemble the troops from Member States. By that time, the genocide was over. While it took six months for the United Nations to assemble its UNAMIR peacekeeping force, it took the perpetrators of Rwanda's genocide only a hundred days to kill over 800,000 people. Millions more fled to the surrounding countries.

In the months after the genocide, UNAMIR peacekeepers continued to function to the best of their abilities in Rwanda, helping refugees resettle, clearing land mines, and paving the way for humanitarian aid. But nothing could undo the unimaginable atrocity that had occurred while the rest of the world did nothing. In 1996, UNAMIR was withdrawn at Rwanda's request. At the end of UNAMIR's mission, the United States had the distinction of being one of the UN Member States who never contributed military or civilian police personnel to Rwanda.

UNMIBH

While the UN's peacekeeping effort in Rwanda was the organization's most notable failure, the United Nations Mission in Bosnia and Herzegovina (UNMIBH) is celebrated as one of its successes. In the early 1990s, as Rwanda was descending into chaos in Africa, a similar situation was happening in a troubled land in Europe. In the area known as the Balkans, long-suppressed ethnic tensions were rising to the surface and boiling over in violence.

Since the time of the Roman Empire, the Balkans have been fought over, conquered, and divided by neighboring lands. As surrounding empires expanded and contracted, the Balkans became ethnically and religiously mixed. The main ethnicities are Serbian (who are mostly Orthodox Christians), Croatian (mainly Catholics), ethnic Albanian (usually Muslims), Slovenian (mostly Catholic), Macedonian (who are largely Orthodox Christians), and Bosniak (who are mostly Muslim). After the First World War, the Balkan lands and peoples were united under one nation, which was eventually named Yugoslavia.

Yugoslavia was never free of ethnic tensions, but for many years its iron-fisted leader, Josip Tito, kept the country united and opposition suppressed. After his death in 1980, the country's nature as a land of divided peoples resurfaced, and the nation began to break apart. The new leader, Serbian Slobodan Milosevic, did nothing to promote peace and unity in the land. In fact, he fueled the fires of hatred, especially in the province of Kosovo where ethnic Albanians far outnumbered Serbs.

In 1991, the federation officially dissolved when Slovenia, Croatia, Bosnia and Herzegovina, and Macedonia declared their independence. Milosevic responded by sending his Serbian army to secure some of the breakaway lands. However, Macedonia's independence went unchallenged by Milosevic. In Slovenia, the army was repelled within ten days. In Croatia and Bosnia and Herzegovina, however, the large Serbian minority population formed an armed resistance backed by the Serbian military. Fighting continued for four years, and atrocious war crimes were committed.

In 1992, the conflict in former Yugoslavia caught the world's attention when Serbian forces invaded and seized Bosnia and Herzegovina's capital city, Sarajevo. Serbian snipers who shot civilians, even thousands of children, kept the city under siege. Then came the "ethnic cleansing." Serbian forces began rounding up the Bosniak population. Some were made to leave their towns and move to other areas. Others were forced into concentration camps. Still others were killed and buried in mass graves. As in Rwanda, peacekeepers (in this case members of the United Nations Protection Force [UNPROFOR]), again charged to only use their weapons in self-defense and hopelessly outnumbered, were largely helpless. By the time a peace agreement was reached in late 1995, more than 200,000 people had been killed, and approximately two million had fled their homes as refugees.

The UNPROFOR mission that operated during the conflict cannot be called a success. However, UNMIBH, which was launched after the peace agreement was signed, had different results. Although UNMIBH was responsible for a variety of tasks in Bosnia and Herzegovina, including humanitarian relief, refugee assistance, demining, setting up elections, and more, its main focus was to assist in reforming the corrupt local police force and helping to build a judicial system that would promote peace, order, and a civil society. In the summary of the report submitted by the secretary-general to the Security Council in 2002, the local police force in Bosnia at the outset of the UNMIBH mission is described in this way:

> Numbering over 44,000—three times peacetime strength—the local police forces were mono-ethnic paramilitary units, organized in three parallel structures, and entirely unsuited to civilian law enforcement. Instead of attempting to provide citizens of minority groups with some sense of security, police forces continued to discriminate against, harass and intimidate citizens who were not of their own ethnicity. Reinforcing the ethnic divisions, freedom of movement was non-existent, blocked by police checkpoints along the Inter-Entity Boundary Line and between communities in the Federation. Moreover, police forces were corrupt and politically dominated.

Houses in Croatia destroyed by the violence of the 1990s

Secretary-General Kofi Annan

At its height, UNMIBH had 2,047 civilian police and military liaison personnel, and hundreds of international and local staff members. It suffered seventeen fatalities: one military personnel, fourteen civilian police officers, and two local civilian staff members. UNMIBH was ended in 2002, when it was decided that the tasks entrusted to the mission had been successfully completed. At the conclusion of the mission, UN Secretary-General Kofi Annan stated:

Through UNMIBH, the United Nations has demonstrated its ability to complete a complex mandate in accordance with a strategic plan and within a realistic and finite time frame. UNMIBH has completed the most extensive police reform and restructuring project ever undertaken by the United Nations.

The United Nations continues its work to build peace around the world.

Chapter

5

UN Peace Missions Today

Today, approximately seventy Special and Personal Representatives and Envoys of the Secretary-General are posted around the world. Their offices are stationed in the Democratic Republic of the Congo, the Horn of Africa, Sudan, Haiti, Afghanistan, Myanmar, Kosovo, Iraq, and many other hot spots in need of UN representatives who can help maintain peaceful negotiations in crisis situations. In addition to these representatives and envoys, the United Nations currently oversees ten political and peace-building missions. Five are in Africa, two are in the Middle East, and three are in Asia and the Pacific.

Extreme poverty, serious health challenges, numerous military conflicts, and other pressing issues are widespread in Africa. For this reason, Africa is often called a "continent in crisis." It is understandable, then, that so many UN political and peace-building missions are focused there. Currently, five of these missions are operational on the continent. They are the United Nations Peace-building Office in the Central African Republic (BONUCA), the Office of the Special Representative of the Secretary-General for the Great Lakes Region, the United Nations Peace-building Support Office in Guinea-Bissau (UNOGBIS), the United Nations Political Office for Somalia (UNPOS), and the Office of the Special Representative of the Secretary-General for West Africa. Of these missions, BONUCA is the largest.

BONUCA

BONUCA was created in February 2000. In the 1990s, the Central African Republic faced a series of attempted military takeovers of its government. The peacekeeping mission, MINURCA, operated from 1998 to 2000 to make the nation's capital, Bangui, secure for a democratically elected government. On MINURCA's completion, BONUCA was put into effect.

Today, the BONUCA peace-building mission faces many challenges. Military groups continue to make attempts to overthrow the government. A collapsed socioeconomic infrastructure leaves many people poor, uneducated, and with little or no means for improving their situation. Even people who work for the government and the military often go without paychecks because the government simply does not have the money to pay all its employees. Furthermore, the ongoing civil war in neighboring Democratic Republic of the Congo sends both refugees and weapons into the region, adding further stresses to the already unstable nation.

Some of the responsibilities of BONUCA are to provide legal assistance to human-rights victims, promote disarmament efforts of armed groups in the region, monitor the region for signs of new instabilities, and work with UN financial and development institutions like the World Bank to create economic opportunities. The Central African Republic is a prime example of why UN peace-building missions are necessary to create the stable and prosperous conditions that allow long-term peace to take hold. The mission currently consists of twenty-three international civilian workers, five military advisers, six civilian police, forty-four local civilian workers, and one UN volunteer.

An African slum; Africa's poverty is one of the reasons why it is often called a "continent in crisis."

The Iraqi flag; the United Nations is helping the Iraqi government get back on its feet after years of violence.

UNAMI

Today the United Nations heads two political/peace-building missions in the Middle East: the Office of the United Nations Special Coordinator for the Middle East (UNSCO) and the United Nations Assistance Mission for Iraq (UNAMI). UNAMI is currently the largest UN political/peace-building mission anywhere in the world.

UNAMI was created in response to the chaotic situation that has descended on Iraq in the wake of the U.S.-led war. In March 2003, the United States, Britain, and a coalition of other countries attacked Iraq. The military action came after the United States **lobbied** the UN Security Council for months for a resolution that would authorize the use of force to dismantle Saddam Hussein's regime. The United States claimed Iraq had weapons of mass destruction and suggested there was evidence Iraq was linked to the September 11, 2001, attacks on the World Trade Center and Pentagon. The sought-after resolution was not granted, and the United States and its allies moved forward without UN support.

The initial war lasted only a few weeks, but it devastated the country's social, economic, political, and physical infrastructures. To make matters worse, into this destruction settled a strong **insurgency** movement, which appears to target not only personnel associated with the military action but anyone (including Iraqi civilians) attempting to participate in the rebuilding of the country, especially the government and the police force. The situation in Iraq is perhaps the greatest peace-building challenge the United Nations and the world has ever seen.

UNAMI began its official operations on September 1, 2003. Some of its main purposes are to advise the Iraqi government on the holding of elections, the drafting of a constitution, the development and rebuilding of civil and social services, and the conducting of a census. UNAMI also assists in the process of reconstruction, promoting new development, providing humanitarian assistance, promoting and protecting human rights, and building a functional judicial system.

Current Peacekeeping Missions

Although peace-building missions like BONUCA and UNAMI are now an important focus for the United Nations, peacekeeping missions continue to be a focal point for the promotion of peace and security around the world. Currently there are sixteen peacekeeping missions operating across the globe: eight African peacekeeping missions are in Sudan, Burundi, Côte d'Ivoire, Liberia, the Democratic Republic of the Congo, Ethiopia and Eritrea, Sierra Leone, and Western Sahara; one peacekeeping mission is operating in the Americas in Haiti; the one peacekeeping

UN peacekeeping forces won a Nobel Peace Prize in 1988.

mission in Asia and the Pacific is the operation between India and Pakistan; three missions are operational in Europe, one in Cyprus, one in Georgia, and one in Kosovo; and the Middle East is home to three missions—in the Golan Heights, Lebanon, and the Middle East.

UNMIS

The United Nations Mission in Sudan (UNMIS) began in March 2005 in response to continued hostilities and gross human-rights violations taking place within the country.

Sudan has only been independent for about fifty years, and for most of that time, it has been a country in conflict. Most of the fighting is between the north and the south of the country. These conflicts are largely ethnically based, arising between the majority Arab-origin Sudanese and the minority African-origin Sudanese.

The United Nations sees the ongoing conflicts in Sudan as a threat to overall world peace. Fighting within the country has led to the death of more than two million people; four million

UN peacekeepers can be recognized by their blue helmets.

Farm-based communities in Darfur are at odds with Arab nomadic communities over land rights.

people were forced from their homes; and 600,000 people fled to other countries as refugees. Furthermore, the Sudanese government has performed numerous actions to anger the international community, including harboring Osama bin Laden and *fundamentalist* organizations in the 1990s.

The most recent conflict in Sudan has been focused in the Darfur region in the western part of the country. The Sudanese government began targeting the region in early 2003, after rebels of the Sudan Liberation Army (SLA) and the Justice and Equality Movement (JEM) attacked government targets claiming Darfur was being neglected. The SLA and JEM are composed mostly of African Sudanese from tribes who live in farming communities. In Darfur, these farm-based communities have long been at odds over land and grazing rights with the mostly *nomadic* Arab communities.

In the attempt to quell the rebel movement, the government enlisted the help of Arab *militias*. The most notorious of these is the Janjaweed. The Sudanese government claims not to have made any agreements with the Janjaweed, but the events in Darfur suggest a different story.

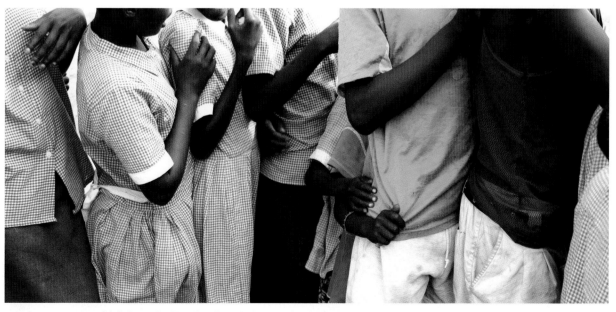

Children in Darfur lived through violent rebel movements in 2003.

At a protest march in March 2004, Americans objected to their government's involvement in the Haitian conflict.

According to Darfur refugees, the Sudanese government was targeting not just rebels but civilians, and the Janjaweed and Arab militias were taking advantage of the situation to drive the African farming communities from the region. The government conducted air raids, and then the Janjaweed stormed on horseback and camels into villages. They rounded up the residents, killed all the men, raped women, stole anything of value, and set fire to what remained. The survivors were driven from their homes and began to congregate in camps near larger towns.

The camps, however, have virtually no food, water, or firewood, and the Janjaweed continue to kill men and rape women they find looking for these necessities outside the camps. The United States has called the events in Darfur genocide, but the United Nations has stopped short of labeling the situation with this term.

So far the Sudanese government has done little to improve the situation in Darfur. It has agreed to disarm the Janjaweed, but has not put the promise into action. A cease-fire has been signed between the government and the SLA, but the situation remains unstable. UNMIS is meant to provide support as the country embarks on what will be a long and difficult journey toward restructuring its government and hopefully one day achieving long-term peace.

Tasks entrusted to UNMIS include monitoring the cease-fire agreement and investigating violations of the agreement; assisting in disarmament; assisting in the creation of a public-information campaign to promote the peace process; assisting in the reform, development, and training of the civilian police force; promoting and monitoring human rights; providing support for the conducting of free and fair elections; and helping with the voluntary return and resettlement of refugees. As of August 2005, UNMIS consisted of 1,926 uniformed personnel (including 1,708 troops), 148 military observers, 70 civilian police, 471 international civilian personnel, 694 local civilian volunteers, and 48 UN volunteers.

MINUSTAH

The United Nations Stabilization Mission in Haiti (MINUSTAH) was authorized in June 2004 after a severe period of political turbulence threatened both that country and the region around it. Although Haiti has a long history of instability, the most recent unrest in Haiti began in 2000, when President Jean-Bertrand Aristide and his Fanmi Lavalas party claimed victory in the presidential and parliamentary elections despite a voter turnout of little more than 10 percent—too little, many felt, to constitute a legitimate election. The government was suspected of tampering with the election results, and formerly separate opposition groups began to unite around one goal: ousting Aristide. By January 2004, with Aristide refusing to resign and the opposition refusing to accept the proposals for reform, the country was in political crisis.

A view of the Golan Heights, site of the ongoing conflict between Israel and Palestine

In February, the political crisis dissolved into armed conflict when insurgents seized control, first of a number of cities, and then of the northern portion of the country. By the end of the month, the insurgency marching toward the capital, Aristide resigned and fled the country.

According to Haitian law, if something happens to the president, the president of the Supreme Court will take over presidential duties until new elections can be held. Then president of the Supreme Court, Boniface Alexander, was sworn in as president within hours of Aristide's departure, and one of his first acts as president was to request assistance from the United Nations.

With the assistance of the United Nations, a transitional government was formed, plans for a 2005 election were made, and the Consensus on the Political Transition Pact was signed. In the pact, the transitional government and other ***signatories*** agreed to take steps toward improving security, promoting development, reforming the judiciary, cracking down on corruption, and other measures that will be important to the long-term stability of Haiti.

MINUSTAH has many responsibilities in Haiti, some of the most important of which are to support the transitional government as it works toward developing a stable, sustainable, and constitutional political process; assist in the reform of the national police force; assist in disarmament;

and assist in the promotion and protection of human rights. As of August 2005, MINUSTAH consisted of 6,263 military troops, 1,401 civilian police, 423 international civilian personnel, about 443 local civilian staff, and 147 UN volunteers. It has suffered eight fatalities: six military personnel, one civilian police officer, and one local civilian staff member.

UNTSO

Although the term "peacekeeping" was not officially used until 1956, the United Nations' very first peacekeeping operation is also its longest running; it began in May 1948, and it is still being carried out today. Located in the Middle East, the mission is called UNTSO—United Nations Truce Supervision Organization. When it began, UNTSO's main purpose was to supervise the observance of the truce in Palestine.

Palestine has for centuries been the site of conflict between religious and political groups. In 1947, the UN General Assembly called for action it hoped would bring an end to these conflicts. It proposed Palestine be divided into two separate states, one Arab and one Jewish. The city of Jerusalem, which is considered holy by both faiths, would be given international status. The Palestinian Arabs and Arab states in the region wanted no part in the plan, and when the State of Israel was proclaimed in May 1948, hostilities immediately ensued. Approximately two weeks later, the UN Security Council called for a truce in Palestine, and military observers were soon sent to the area. A strong peacekeeping force has been present in the region ever since.

UNTSO personnel work not only within Israel and Palestinian territory, but also with the neighboring Arab countries of Egypt, Jordan, Lebanon, and the Syrian Arab Republic. The region remains *volatile*; wars broke out in 1956, 1967, and 1973, and conflicts requiring UN intervention continue to arise. At its height, UNTSO had nearly 700 military observers. It currently consists of 151 military observers, 101 international civilian personnel, and 120 local civilian staff. To date, it has suffered forty-one fatalities.

A Chronology of Peacekeeping Missions

May 1948–present: UNTSO (United Nations Truce Supervision Organization), Middle East

January 1949–present: UNMOGIP (United Nations Military Observer Group in India and Pakistan)

November 1956–June 1967: UNEF I (First United Nations Emergency Force), Middle East

June–December 1958: UNOGIL (United Nations Observation Group in Lebanon)

July 1960–June 1964: ONUC (United Nations Operation in the Congo)

October 1962–April 1963: UNSF (United Nations Security Force in West New Guinea)

July 1963–September 1964: UNYOM (United Nations Yemen Observation Mission)

March 1964–present: UNFICYP (United Nations Peacekeeping Force in Cyprus)

May 1965–October 1966: DOMREP (Mission of the Representative of the Secretary–General in the Dominican Republic)

September 1965–March 1966: UNIPOM (United Nations India–Pakistan Observation Mission)

October 1973–July 1979: UNEF II (Second United Nations Emergency Force), Middle East

May 1974–present: UNDOF (United Nations Disengagement Observer Force), Golan Heights

March 1978–present: UNIFIL (United Nations Interim Force in Lebanon)

May 1988–March 1990: UNGOMAP (United Nations Good Offices Mission in Afghanistan and Pakistan)

August 1988–February 1991: UNIIMOG (United Nations Iran–Iraq Military Observer Group)

December 1988–May 1991: UNAVEM I (United Nations Angola Verification Mission I)

April 1989–March 1990: UNTAG (United Nations Transition Assistance Group), Namibia

November 1989–January 1992: ONUCA (United Nations Observer Group in Central America)

April 1991–October 2003: UNIKOM (United Nations Iraq–Kuwait Observation Mission)

April 1991–present: MINURSO (United Nations Mission for the Referendum in Western Sahara)

May 1991–February 1995: UNAVEM II (United Nations Angola Verification Mission II)

July 1991–April 1995: ONUSAL (United Nations Observer Mission in El Salvador)

October 1991–March 1992: UNAMIC (United Nations Advance Mission in Cambodia)

February 1992–September 1993: UNTAC (United Nations Transitional Authority in Cambodia)

February 1992–March 1995: UNPROFOR (United Nations Protection Force), former Yugoslavia

April 1992–March 1993: UNOSOM I (United Nations Operation in Somalia I)

December 1992–December 1994: ONUMOZ (United Nations Operation in Mozambique)

March 1993–March 1995: UNOSOM II (United Nations Operation in Somalia II)

June 1993–September 1994: UNOMUR (United Nations Observer Mission Uganda–Rwanda)

August 1993–present: UNOMIG (United Nations Observer Mission in Georgia)

September 1993–June 1996: UNMIH (United Nations Mission in Haiti)

September 1993–September 1997: UNOMIL (United Nations Observer Mission in Liberia)

October 1993–March 1996: UNAMIR (United Nations Assistance Mission for Rwanda)

May–June 1994: UNASOG (United Nations Aouzou Strip Observer Group), Chad and Libya

December 1994–May 2000: UNMOT (United Nations Mission of Observers in Tajikistan)

February 1995–June 1997: UNAVEM III (United Nations Angola Verification Mission III)

March 1995–January 1996: UNCRO (United Nations Confidence Restoration Operation), Croatia

March 1995–February 1999: UNPREDEP (United Nations Preventive Deployment Force), former Yugoslav Republic of Macedonia

December 1995–December 2002: UNMIBH (United Nations Mission in Bosnia and Herzegovina)

January 1996–January 1998: UNTAES (United Nations Transitional Authority in Eastern Slavonia, Baranja and Western Sirmium), Croatia

February 1996–December 2002: UNMOP (United Nations Mission of Observers in Prevlaka), Croatia and the Federal Republic of Yugoslavia

July 1996–July 1997: UNSMIH (United Nations Support Mission in Haiti)

January–May 1997: MINUGUA (United Nations Verification Mission in Guatemala)

June 1997–February 1999: MONUA (United Nations Observer Mission in Angola)

August–November 1997: UNTMIH (United Nations Transition Mission in Haiti)

December 1997–March 2000: MIPONUH (United Nations Civilian Police Mission in Haiti)

January 1998–October 1998: UNPSG (United Nations Civilian Police Support Group), Croatia

April 1998–February 2000: MINURCA (United Nations Mission in the Central African Republic)

July 1998–October 1999: UNOMSIL (United Nations Observer Mission in Sierra Leone)

June 1999–present: UNMIK (United Nations Interim Administration Mission in Kosovo)

October 1999–May 2002: UNTAET (United Nations Transitional Administration in East Timor)

October 1999–present: UNAMSIL (United Nations Mission in Sierra Leone)

November 1999–present: MONUC (United Nations Organization Mission in the Democratic Republic of the Congo)

July 2000–present: UNMEE (United Nations Mission in Ethiopia and Eritrea)

May 2002–May 2005: UNMISET (United Nations Mission of Support in East Timor)

September 2003–present: UNMIL (United Nations Mission in Liberia)

April 2004–present: UNOCI (United Nations Operation in Côte d'Ivoire)

June 2004–present: MINUSTAH (United Nations Stabilization Mission in Haiti)

June 2004–present: ONUB (United Nations Operation in Burundi)

March 2005–present: UNMIS (United Nations Mission in the Sudan)

Time Line

June 12, 1941	Declaration of St. James's Palace is signed in London.
January 1, 1942	The United Nations Declaration is signed.
June 26, 1945	Charter of the United Nations is signed in San Francisco.
October 24, 1945	Charter of the United Nations officially goes into effect.
1946	International Court of Justice is founded.
1947	United Nations proposes Palestine be divided into two states, one Arab and one Jewish.
May 1948	State of Israel is proclaimed; hostilities immediately ensue in Middle East; the first United Nations peacekeeping mission is launched in the Middle East.
1955	Last year in which United Nations suffers no peacekeeping fatalities.
January 1, 1956	Sudan gains independence from United Kingdom.
July 1956	Egyptian President Nasser nationalizes Suez Canal companies.
October 1956	Security Council passes resolution on the running of the Suez Canal.
October 29, 1956	Israel invades Egypt; British and French troops soon follow.
November 1956	UNEF I goes into affect to assist in cessation of hostilities in Egypt; it is the first time the term "peacekeeping" is used.
1962	Rwanda becomes independent from Belgium; Hutus gain control of government.
June 5–11, 1967	Six-day war between Israel and Egypt.

1968	Countries begin signing the Treaty on the Non-Proliferation of Nuclear Weapons.
October 6, 1973	Yom Kippur War begins with Egyptian and Syrian attacks on Israel.
1980	Yugoslavia's president, Josip Tito, dies.
1990	Rwandan Patriotic Front begins invading Rwanda from Uganda.
1991	Slovenia, Croatia, Bosnia and Herzegovina, and Macedonia declare independence from Yugoslavia.
April 6, 1992	Serb sniper attacks begin in Sarajevo, capital of Bosnia and Herzegovina.
July 1992	Cease-fire is called between Rwandan Patriotic Front and Rwandan government.
February 1993	Hostilities resume in Rwanda.
August 1993	Peace agreement is signed in Rwanda.
April 6, 1994	Rwandan president is killed when his plane is shot down; within hours, the killing of Tutsis and moderate Hutus begins.
November 1, 1994	Trusteeship Council suspends regular operation.
December 14, 1995	Peace agreement is signed in former Yugoslavia.
1996	Countries begin signing the Comprehensive Nuclear-Test-Ban Treaty.
1997	Countries begin signing the Convention on the Prohibition of the Use, Stockpiling, Production and Transfer of Antipersonnel Mines and on Their Destruction.
November 26, 2000	President Aristide of Haiti is reelected in controversial elections.
February 2000	United Nations Peace-building Office in the Central African Republic opens.

September 11, 2001	Terrorists attack World Trade Center and Pentagon.
February 2003	Sudan Liberation Army and Justice and Equality Movement rebels in Darfur region begin attacking government targets; government retaliation with air raids and government-backed militias begins soon after.
March 2003	U.S.-led coalition forces attack Iraq.
September 1, 2003	United Nations Assistance Mission for Iraq begins.
February 2004	Armed uprising begins in Haiti; by end of month, President Aristide resigns and flees the country.
2006	MINUSTAH works for peace in Haiti; UNTSO continues its work in the Middle East.

Glossary

civil law: The law of a state dealing with the rights of private citizens.

consensus: Widespread agreement among members of a group.

diplomatic: Concerned with international diplomacy—the practice of using negotiations rather than force to settle conflicts between nations—or the work of diplomats, those people who carry out such negotiations.

disarmament: The process of reducing a nation's supply of weapons or the strength of its armed forces.

embargos: Government restrictions on trade in a particular commodity or with a particular nation.

envoys: People who act as diplomats on behalf of a national government.

escalating: Worsening.

fundamentalist: Person who believes in the strict adherence to a doctrine or religious belief.

genocide: The systematic killing of all people from a national, ethnic, or religious group, or an attempt at such killing.

humanitarian: Concerned with the well-being of others.

insurgency: A rebellion or uprising against a government.

liaison: Go-between.

lobbied: Campaigned to influence a politician.

maritime: Relating to the sea or shipping.

militias: Civilian soldiers who take military training and can serve full time during an emergency.

nomadic: Moving from place to place, with no permanent home, often on a seasonal basis.

parliament: A legislative body.

preamble: A section at the beginning of a speech or formal document that explains the purpose of what follows.

propaganda: Information or publicity put out by an organization or government to spread and promote a policy.

sanctions: Economic or military coercive measures adopted usually by several nations together to force a nation violating international law to stop its actions.

signatories: Persons or governments who have signed a treaty and are bound by it.

states: Areas with their own governments and legislatures; countries, nations.

sustainable: Relating to a method of using a resource so that the resource is not depleted or permanently damaged.

vested: Having an unquestionable right to the possession of a property or a privilege.

veto: To reject something.

visionary: Characterized by unusually acute foresight and imagination.

volatile: Prone to sudden change.

Further Reading

Barnett, Michael. *Eyewitness to a Genocide: The United Nations and Rwanda.* New York: Cornell University Press, 2003.

Connolly, Sean. *United Nations: Keeping the Peace.* Chicago, Ill.: Raintree Library, 2003.

Fasulo, Linda. *An Insider's Guide to the UN.* New York: Yale University Press, 2003.

Johnson, Edward. *United Nations—Peacekeeper?* New York: Thomson Learning, 2005.

Meisler, Stanley. *United Nations: The First Fifty Years.* Boston: Atlantic Monthly Press, 2000.

Melvern, Linda. *United Nations.* Danbury, Conn.: Franklin Watts, 2001.

Schlesinger, Stephen C. *Act of Creation: The Founding of the United Nations: A Story of Superpowers, Secret Agents, Wartime Allies and Enemies, and Their Quest for a Peaceful World.* New York: Westview Press, 2003.

United Nations. *Basic Facts About the United Nations.* New York: Bernan Press, 2004.

For More Information

Charter of the United Nations
www.un.org/aboutun/charter/index.html

The International Campaign to Ban Landmines
www.icbl.org

Karuna Center for Peacebuilding
www.karunacenter.org

The Partnership for Effective Peacekeeping
www.effectivepeacekeeping.org

The United Nations
www.un.org

United Nations Department of Peacekeeping Operations
www.un.org/Depts/dpko/dpko/index.asp

United Nations Department of Political Affairs
www.un.org/Depts/dpa/index.htm

United Nations Peacekeeping Best Practices
pbpu.unlb.org/pbpu

United States Institute of Peace
www.usip.org

Publisher's note:
The Web sites listed on this page were active at the time of publication. The publisher is not responsible for Web sites that have changed their addresses or discontinued operation since the date of publication. The publisher will review and update the Web-site list upon each reprint.

Reports and Projects

Meeting of the General Assembly
Hold a General Assembly meeting in your classroom. Begin by having the class vote to choose a student who will be the secretary-general. That student will research the UN's current secretary-general. Assign a country to each of the other students. The students will research the current affairs of their countries. Topics to pay particular attention to may include threats to peace and security, the environment, human rights, and international relations. Hold your General Assembly meeting. The secretary-general will open the meeting by, playing the part of the current UN secretary-general, presenting his or her resume to the assembly. Then each country will give a report to the General Assembly about its current challenges. Have the secretary-general facilitate a discussion regarding which challenges warrant UN intervention and what UN body the issue should be referred to (for example, should the situation be dealt with in the Economic and Social Council, the Security Council, the International Court of Justice, etc.). Hold a General Assembly vote after the discussions.

Meeting of the Security Council
Assign a country that is a current member of the Security Council to individual students or pairs of students. Pick an issue that has gone before the Security Council in the past. Have the students research the issue from both general and their countries' specific points of view. Hold a Security Council meeting where students will debate the issue and then vote on a resolution. Now have the students research a current conflict in the world that the Security Council has not yet passed a resolution on. Hold another Security Council meeting. Debate the issue and attempt to come to a resolution.

Reports and Presentations on Secretary-Generals
Divide the class into groups. Have each group research one of the UN's secretary-generals. Each group will then write a biography of their secretary-general and make a presentation to the class. Main topics should include childhood, education, career (pre- and post-UN), and major accomplishments.

Reports and Presentations on Peacekeeping Missions
Have each student choose a peacekeeping mission that was not discussed in depth in this book. Students should research and make a presentation on the history of the conflict, the events that triggered UN intervention, the mission, and the probability of long-term peace in the future.

Bibliography

Bellamy, J. Alex, Paul Williams, and Stuart Griffin. *Understanding Peacekeeping.* Cambridge, United Kingdom: Polity Press, 2004.

Connolly, Sean. *United Nations: Keeping the Peace.* Chicago, Ill.: Raintree Library, 2003.

Dallaire, Roméo. *Shake Hands with the Devil: The Failure of Humanity in Rwanda.* New York: Carroll & Graf Publishers, 2003.

Diehl, Paul F. *International Peacekeeping.* Baltimore, Md.: Johns Hopkins University Press, 2004.

Jacobs, William Jay. *Search for Peace: The Story of the United Nations.* Old Tappan, N.J.: Charles Scribner's Sons, 2004.

Patterson, Charles. *The Oxford 50th Anniversary Book of the United Nations.* New York: Oxford University Press, 1995.

Ross, Stewart. *United Nations.* Chicago, Ill.: Raintree Library, 2003.

Thakur, Ramesh, and Albrecht Schnabel, eds. *United Nations Peacekeeping Operations: Ad Hoc Missions, Permanent Engagement.* New York: United Nations University Press, 2002.

Index

Picture Credits

Biographies

Author

Autumn Libal earned her bachelor of arts from Smith College in Northampton, Massachusetts. She is the author of numerous educational books for young people. Other Mason Crest series she has written for include the European Union: Political, Social, and Economic Cooperation, Women's Issues: Global Trends, North American Indians Today, and Hispanic Heritage.

Series Consultant

Bruce Russett is Dean Acheson Professor of Political Science at Yale University and editor of the *Journal of Conflict Resolution*. He has taught or researched at Columbia, Harvard, M.I.T., Michigan, and North Carolina in the United States, and educational institutions in Belgium, Britain, Israel, Japan, and the Netherlands. He has been president of the International Studies Association and the Peace Science Society, holds an honorary doctorate from Uppsala University in Sweden. He was principal adviser to the U.S. Catholic Bishops for their pastoral letter on nuclear deterrence in 1985, and co-directed the staff for the 1995 Ford Foundation Report, *The United Nations in Its Second Half Century*. He has served as editor of the *Journal of Conflict Resolution* since 1973. The twenty-five books he has published include *The Once and Future Security Council* (1997), *Triangulating Peace: Democracy, Interdependence, and International Organizations* (2001), *World Politics: The Menu for Choice* (8th edition 2006), and *Purpose and Policy in the Global Community* (2006).